Table of Contents

Address:
South Africa, 0700 Polokwane, 0742 Seshego zone6 109,
St Khensani drive 247
Phone: 0725438106
Email: khomotjomashita@gmail.com
Website: N/A
Title: The African Warrior
Author: Khomotjo Peter Mashita
Self-Published
About the Author:
Khomotjo Peter Mashita is a South African author and entrepreneur. He is passionate about African history and culture and has woven his interests into his debut novel, The African Warrior.

The African Warrior (son of the soil)
Historical Fiction
Khomotso Mashita

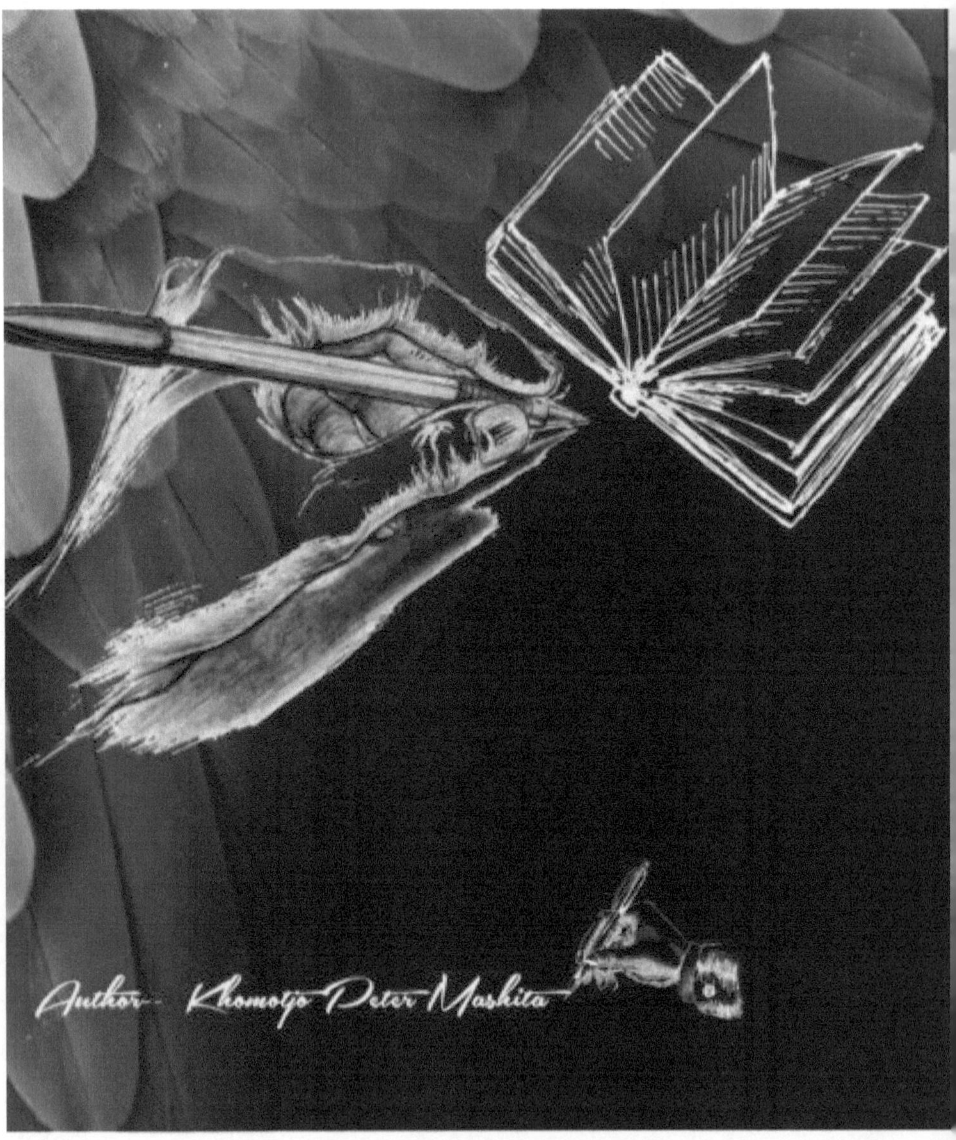

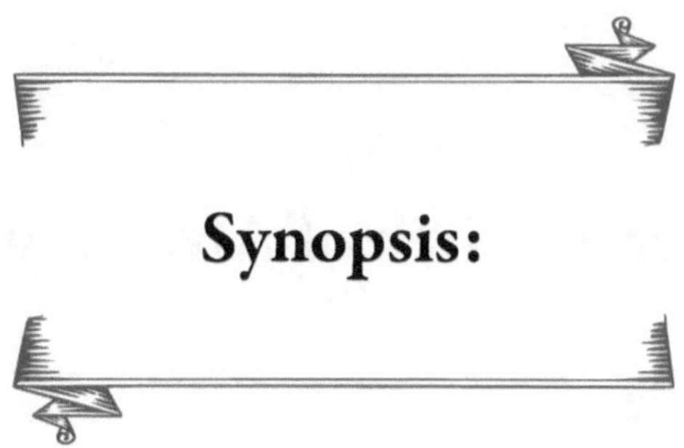

Synopsis:

The African Warrior follows the story of Khomotso, a fierce warrior from a small village in southern Africa. He was born with a pure strand of white hair on his right side and a mark on his right hand as prophesied in the heart of Africa. From a young age, Khomotso showed signs of great natural strength and a hunger for knowledge. He discovered a forbidden tree that granted him immense powers, which he used to become a renowned warrior and defend his people and land against other tribes and white colonizers. Khomotso was also a loving husband and father who trained his children to master their abilities. He became a legend in his own time and a symbol of strength and hope for his tribe. The story is set in Africa, a world of diverse cultures, traditions, and histories, where courage, strength, and family bonds are highly valued. He fought against neighbouring tribes and colonizers, Khomotso used all his skills and super abilities to protect his

people and reclaim his home.

The African Warrior is a symbol of strength, courage, resilience and ability to survive and thrive in the face of adversity.

The African Warrior is a symbol of the African people's determination to fight for their freedom, protect their rights and injustice. It is people's determination to stand up for what is right and to fight for what is just.

Chapter 1: Birth of African warrior

Once upon a time, in a small village (Seshego) in the heart of Africa, There lived warrior named Khomotso from Mashita tribe known as Bapedi tribe today. He was said to be born in the far country of South Africa-Limpopo, he was the only son from his parents Kgaugelo (Father) and Naledi (mother). Khomotso was born during the reign of king Kgoroshi in the year 1683(AD).

King Kgoroshi was a black tall and regal man, with broad shoulders and a commanding presence. He had a square jaw and piercing brown eyes, which he used to great effect when addressing his courtiers and advisors. His hair was thick and black.

Despite his height, Kgoroshi was slender and lithe, with a grace and agility that belied his years. He moved with a quiet confidence, and was often seen wearing izicolo (hart) and leopard skin spoke to his status as a king.

Despite his imposing stature and reputation as a warrior, Kgoroshi was known for his kindness and generosity towards his people. He was often seen visiting the sick and the poor, and was always willing to listen to the concerns of his subjects. His commitment to his people was unwavering, and he was beloved by many as a fair and just ruler.

King Kgoroshi was a man of noble birth, born into a family with a long history of rulership over their people. However, despite his privileged position, Kgoroshi was also known to be a weak and indecisive ruler. He was easily swayed by his advisors and courtiers, and was often unable to make tough decisions that would benefit his kingdom.

Khomotso, the child of prophecy, was born during Kgoroshi's reign. Though the king was initially sceptical of the boy's supposed destiny, he could not deny reality and the signs. Kgoroshi watched as Khomotso grew into a strong and fearless warrior, with a deep sense of justice and a fierce loyalty to his people.

Khomotso was born into a world of struggle and suffering. His tribe had been at war with neighboring tribes for generations, and the constant fighting had taken its toll on the people. Food was scarce, and disease was rampant. But even in the midst of all this hardship, Khomotso's parents were determined to give their son a better life.

But life was not easy for Khomotso, He watched as his friends and family members dying from disease and starvation. He saw the toll that war was taking on his people, and he knew that something had to be done.

One night when he was 11 years old, Khomotso had a vision. He saw a powerful spirit of tall grey bearded black man with bald head; his eyes were like lazing fire. He told him that he is destined for greatness. The spirit told him that he had been chosen to be a warrior of the people, a protector of his tribe and all of Africa.

Khomotso woke up the next morning with a newfound sense of purpose. He knew that he had to train and become strong to fight and protect his people.

Chapter 2: The Warrior's Early Years

Khomotso's parents were simple farmers, and they had no idea that their son was destined for greatness. But the village elders knew. They had seen the signs of the apocalypse because it was said that the child of prophesy will be born with pure strand of white hair on his right side and a mark on his fore head, and they knew that Khomotso was the one who would fulfil the prophecy.

The prophecy said that a great warrior would be born who would save the people of Africa from a great evil and colonisation. The elders had been waiting for this warrior for 520 years, and when Khomotso was born, they knew that he was the one.

Khomotso grew up in the village, learning the ways of his people. He was a strong and brave boy, and he loved to hunt and fish.

Khomotso's parent raised him to be a strong and brave warrior, teaching him the ways of the spear, bow and the shield.

He was natural at combat, and soon he was the best fighter in the village. He was respected by all, and his parents were proud of him.

At the age of sixteen, Khomotso left his home to join the basic combat training of the kingdom. He was eager to prove himself and to serve his country. He quickly rose through the ranks, becoming respected among his peers.

He passed in many training, and he was always victorious and also known for his courage and skill, and he was often called upon to lead the team. He was a natural leader, and his peers followed him without questions.

The young warrior was eventually promoted to the small rank of soldiers; He was given command of a small rand of soldiers on a mission to protect their village from a neighbouring tribe that had been causing trouble.

Khomotso, a young African warrior, met Tebogo, a girl from a neighbouring village, in the bush while they were both traveling to different destinations.

They instantly connected and spent hours talking and laughing together, were discovering a mutual attraction.

Unfortunately, their time together was brief as they were both forced to continue on their journeys. Khomotso promised to find a way to see Tebogo again, but he had no idea how he would do it.

Days turned into weeks, and weeks turned into months, and Khomotso couldn't stop thinking about Tebogo. He tried asking around his village about her, but nobody seemed to know who she was or where she came from.

Khomotso started to lose hope and resigned himself to the fact that he may never see Tebogo again. But deep down, he knew he could never forget her.

He and his fellow warriors received word that the Swati tribe was planning an attack, and Khomotso knew that they had to act fast.

As they made their way through the dense jungle, Khomotso could feel the tension in the air. He knew that they were getting closer to the enemy, and he could sense that they were being watched.

Suddenly, they heard a rustling in the bushes ahead of them. Khomotso signalled for his soldiers to be ready, and they all drew their bows.

Out of the bushes stepped a group of warriors from the enemy tribe. They were heavily armed and looked ready for battle.

Khomotso stepped forward, and drew his spear. He knew that this was going to be a tough fight, but he was determined to protect his people. The two groups clashed, and the sound of metal on metal echoed through the jungle. Khomotso fought with all his might, his spear blade flashing in the sunlight.

Despite being outnumbered, Khomotso and his soldiers fought bravely. They were determined to protect their village at all costs.

After what seemed like hours, the enemy tribe finally retreated, Khomotso and his soldiers had emerged victorious.

As they made their way back to the village, Khomotso couldn't help but feel proud of his soldiers. They had fought with honour and had protected their people.

He knew that there would be more battles to come, but he was ready for whatever lay ahead and he would do whatever it takes to protect his people and his land.

Chapter 3: The Warrior's Training and forbidden tree

The sun was just beginning to rise over the horizon as the young warrior awoke from his slumber. He had been training for weeks now, and he was determined to make the most of this day. He quickly got dressed and grabbed his spear and shield before heading out to the training grounds.

The training grounds were a large open field with a few trees scattered around. In the centre of the field was a large wooden post with a target painted on it.

The warrior took a deep breath and began his training; He started with basic spear drills, practicing his swings and thrusts. He worked on his footwork, making sure he was always in the correct stance. He worked on his parries and blocks, making sure he was always ready to defend himself.

After a few hours of practice, the warrior was starting to feel more confident in his abilities. He was beginning to understand the basics of spear play and was starting to feel more comfortable with his weapon.

There was a skilled captain in the tribal army called Kgaugelo; He had earned his position through years of hard work and dedication to his craft. He had risen through the ranks quickly, thanks to his natural talent as a warrior and his tireless work ethic.

When the young boy Khomotso was identified as the child of prophecy, it was Kgaugelo who was chosen to train him. The captain knew that this would be no easy task, but he was determined to do whatever it took to help the boy fulfil his destiny.

For months, Kgaugelo worked with Khomotso tirelessly, teaching him everything he knew about strategy, tactics, and hand-to-hand combat. He pushed the boy to his limits, demanding nothing but the best from him at all times.

Despite the intense training, Kgaugelo and Khomotso developed a deep bond, with the captain serving as a mentor and father figure to the young warrior. He shared his own experiences and wisdom with the boy, helping him to understand the complexities of leadership and the importance of compassion and understanding.

As Khomotso grew in skill and confidence, Kgaugelo knew that his work was done. He had done his best to prepare the boy for the challenges that lay ahead, and he was proud to have played a small part in the destiny of one of his people's greatest heroes.

Captain Kgaugelo was a tall and muscular man, with broad shoulders and a chiselled jawline. He had short-dreads hair, which he kept neatly trimmed, and his piercing brown eyes conveyed a sense of wisdom and experience beyond his years.

As a captain in the tribal army, Kgaugelo was highly respected by his fellow soldiers, and was known for his bravery and leadership on the battlefield. He was a skilled fighter, with a deep understanding of tactics and strategy, and was often called upon to lead his men in the most difficult and dangerous missions.

Despite his fearsome reputation as a warrior, Kgaugelo was also known for his kindness and compassion towards his comrades. He was always willing to lend an ear to those who needed to talk, and was quick to offer advice or a helping hand when needed.

When he was tasked with training Khomotso, the child of prophecy, Kgaugelo took the responsibility seriously. He recognized the boy's potential, and worked tirelessly to help him hone his skills as a warrior. He was patient and supportive, but also firm and demanding, pushing Khomotso to his limits in order to unlock his full potential.

The next step in his training was to practice against a real opponent whom it was expected to defeat Khomotso because of his skills and combat experience.

Khomotso had been training with Captain Kgaugelo for months, learning the skills and strategies he would need to fulfil his destiny as the child of prophecy. Each day, he worked tirelessly to hone his abilities, pushing himself to the limits in order to become the best warrior he could be.

One day, Kgaugelo decided to put Khomotso's skills to the test. He challenged the young warrior to a mock battle, with Khomotso armed with his trusty spear and shield, and Kgaugelo long bladed spear and a large shield.

At first, Khomotso was nervous. He had never fought someone as skilled as Kgaugelo before, and he knew that he would need to be at his absolute best in order to stand a chance.

As the battle began, Khomotso was surprised at how quickly his training kicked in. He moved fast, dodging Kgaugelo's attacks and striking back with precise and deadly blows from his spear.

Kgaogelo was impressed. He had trained many warriors over the years, but he had never seen someone as skilled and agile as Khomotso. As the battle continued, Khomotso began to gain the upper hand, slowly wearing down Kgaugelo defences with a flurry of well-placed strikes.

In the end, Khomotso emerged victorious. He had defeated one of the greatest warriors in the land, and had done so with a grace and skill that belied his years.

Kgaugelo was astonished by what he had witnessed. He had seen many warriors in his time, but none as talented as Khomotso. He knew that the boy was destined for greatness, and that he would go on to do great things for his people.

As they left the training ground, Kgaugelo clapped Khomotso on the back. "You are a true warrior, my boy," he said. "Never forget that. You have a destiny to fulfil, and I have no doubt that you will do so with honour and courage."

The next day, after his victory over Captain Kgaugelo, Khomotso was resting in his Indus when he suddenly had a vision. A powerful spirit appeared before him, its form shimmering and shifting in the flickering light of the fire.

"Khomotso," the spirit said, its voice echoing in his mind. "I have come to guide you. Your people are in great danger, and only you can save them."

Khomotso sat up in a vision, his heart pounding with anticipation. "What must I do?" he asked.

The spirit pointed to a distant mountain range, its peaks shrouded in mist. "There is a forbidden tree that grows in those mountains," it said. "It bears a fruit that can grant great power to those who eat it. But it can only be harvested once every ten thousand years, and only by one who is worthy."

When he woke up he was fascinated because of the dream, it reminded him of warrior tales who ate of forbidden tree and absorbed its energy it was said they had super strength and ability to control the elements. He longed to have that kind of power, to be able to protect his people and defeat their enemies.

Khomotso knew what he had to do. He gathered his spear and shield, and set out on a journey to the mountains. For days, he trekked through rugged terrain, facing perilous challenges and overcoming them with his skill and courage. Finally, he arrived at the base of the forbidden tree, it was tall and majestic, with leaves that shimmered in the sunlight. And hanging from one of its branches was a fruit, glowing with an otherworldly light.

Khomotso knew that this was no ordinary fruit. He had heard stories of the forbidden tree of the gods, a tree that only bore fruit once every 10,000 years. The fruit was said to grant incredible powers to whoever ate it, but it was strictly forbidden to mortals.

He remembered the vision he had the words from powerful spirited. He climbed the tree and plucked the fruit from its branch. As he took a bite, he felt a surge of energy coursing through his body. He felt stronger, faster, and more powerful than he ever had before.

At first, Khomotso had felt nothing. But then, he had felt a surge of energy coursing through his body. He had felt stronger, faster, and more powerful than he had ever felt before. The spirit that had guided him to the tree appeared before him once more, and spoke to him in a voice that echoed through his mind.

"You have been granted great power, Khomotso," the spirit said. "But with that power comes great responsibility. You must use your newfound abilities to protect your people, and to bring peace and harmony to the land."

Khomotso nodded in agreement, knowing that he had been given a great gift, and that he would use it wisely.

Chapter 4: Sage superpower training

For weeks, Khomotso had hidden his powers from everyone. He had trained in secret, honing his skills and learning to control his newfound abilities. He had learned to move faster than the eye could see, to jump higher than any mortal, and to strike with the force.

But Khomotso knew that he could not keep his powers hidden forever. He knew that he had to learn to control them before they consumed him.

After a week of Khomotso decided to call Captain Kgaugelo and tell him about his extraordinary experience. The captain was initially sceptical but soon saw for himself the incredible strength and speed that Khomotso possessed. He knew that Khomotso's power was the gods, but it was clear that he needed guidance on how to control it.

Captain Kgaugelo took Khomotso on a journey to the sage Matsebatsohle who lived at the top highest mountain in the land. The sage was a wise and powerful man who had lived for centuries, and he had trained many warriors in the art of combat and control of their powers.

Sage Matsebatsohle was a short, black dark man with deep-set eyes, his eyes pupil was cyan blue in colour and a weathered face that spoke of a lifetime spent atop the mountain. His dreads hair was long and grey and his beard reached down to his chest. Despite his age, he moved with the grace and agility of a much younger man, his every movement precise and deliberate.

Matsebatsohle was known throughout the land as a powerful sage, a man who had lived for centuries and had trained countless warriors in the art of combat and control of their powers. His abilities were said to be legendary, and many warriors sought him out in the hopes of learning from him.

Aside from his incredible mastery of combat, Matsebatsohle was also said to have incredible psychic abilities. It was said that he could read a person's thoughts with a mere glance and that he could sense danger from miles away.

However, his true gift lay in his ability to teach. He had a way of connecting with his students on a deep level, and he was able to bring out the best in them. He pushed them to their limits and beyond, knowing that only through struggle and hardship could they truly become the warriors they were meant to be.

Despite his immense power and knowledge, Matsebatsohle was a humble man who cared deeply for his students. He saw in Khomotso a potential for greatness, and he knew that with his help, he could guide the young warrior to become the protector his people needed.

Matsebatsohle's abilities were truly unmatched, and he was revered by all who knew of him. He lived a simple life atop the mountain, dedicating himself to the art of combat and the training of young warriors, content in the knowledge that he was helping to shape the future of his people.

Upon reaching the top of the mountain, Khomotso and Captain Kgaugelo were greeted by the sage, who welcomed them warmly. The sage knew immediately what had happened to Khomotso and began to teach him how to control his newfound powers.

Kgaugelo left the mountain with a happy heart, knowing that he was leaving Khomotso in good hands; He left him and went back.

Kgaugelo felt a sense of unease as he made his way back to his village. He had a nagging feeling that something was not right, but he couldn't quite put his finger on what it was.

As he approached the outskirts of the village, he saw a group of men gathered around something on the ground. He hurried over to see what was going on, and his heart sank when he saw that it was the lifeless body of one of his fellow villagers.

Kgaugelo knew then that something terrible had happened. He asked the men gathered around what had occurred, and they told him that a group of bandits had attacked the village earlier that day.

Kgaugelo's heart filled with rage at the thought of his people being attacked by such cowardly thugs. He knew that he had to act fast if he was going to save the rest of his village from harm.

He quickly rallied to village protectors and led them in a counter-attack against the bandits from Shona tribe. Kgaugelo was a skilled warrior, and he fought with all his might to protect his people.

The battle raged on for hours, with both sides taking heavy casualties. But in the end, Kgaugelo died in the middle of the battle, Kgaugelo was stabbed in the back with a cultural knife, coated in a deadly poison, but after hours of fighting, Mashita warriors emerged victorious. The bandits were driven off, and the village was saved.

Khomotso was devastated to hear of Captain Kgaugelo's death. He had lost one of his closest friends and mentors, and he felt a deep sense of grief and anger at the injustice of it all.

Despite his grief, Khomotso knew that he could not let his friend's death be in vain. He was now more determined than ever to master his newfound powers and to use them to protect his people.

Khomotso explained everything to Matsebatsohle, after an hour of listening to Khomotso's story. He told Khomotso that he had done a great thing by eating the forbidden fruit. He had said that Khomotso was destined for greatness, but that he needed to learn to control his powers before they destroyed him. And so, Matsebatsohle had taught Khomotso how to meditate and how to focus his mind. He had taught him how to channel his powers and how to use them for good. He had taught him to be patient and to trust in himself.

For months, Khomotso had trained with the sage, learning to control his powers and to use them for good. He had become stronger, faster, and more powerful than ever before. And he had learned that with great power came great responsibility.

Under the tutelage of Sage Matsebatsohle, Khomotso trained tirelessly, honing his skills in combat and learning how to control his lightning-fast speed and immense strength. He also learned how to tap into his psychic abilities, honing his mind and his senses to a razor-sharp edge. He became more and more confident in his abilities. He knew that he was destined for greatness, and he felt a deep sense of purpose and responsibility to use his powers for the good of his people.

But even as he trained with Sage Matsebatsohle, Khomotso could feel the weight of the prophecy on his shoulders. He knew that he was the chosen one, the one who would bring balance to the world and defeat the great evil that threatened to consume it.

With each passing day, Khomotso grew stronger and more powerful. He knew that the time would come when he would have to face his destiny head-on, and he was determined to be ready for whatever challenges lay ahead.

Now Khomotso was ready to use his powers to save his people and to defeat the enemy. He was a warrior and a child of prophecy, and he was ready to fulfil his destiny.

Chapter 5: Death of warrior's parents and his return

He had been gone for nine (9) months and two (2) weeks, while he was fishing in the mountains he saw a bird swoop down and land on a tree. He recognized the bird as one that was often used to deliver messages, and his heart quickened with anticipation.

As he approached the bird, it took flight once again, but not before dropping a small piece of parchment tied to its leg. Khomotso quickly retrieved the parchment and unfolded it, his eyes scanning the words written on it.

The message was short and to the point, but it sent chills down Khomotso's spine. It was short, telling him that his village was under attack by Shona tribe; His parents were killed during the attack.

Khomotso was devastated to hear that his parents had been killed during the attack.

Filled with grief and anger, Khomotso immediately set out to return to his village. He traveled as fast as he could, using his superpowers of strength and lightning speed to cover the distance in record time. When he arrived, he found his village in ruins, with many of the shelters burned to the ground and the remaining villagers hiding in fear.

Khomotso was filled with sorrow as he mourned the loss of his parents. He prepared a traditional burial ceremony for them, with the help of his tribe. The air was filled with the sound of weeping and mourning as Khomotso placed their bodies in the ground.

He remembered his father's words about being a warrior, and he felt a renewed sense of purpose. Khomotso knew that he had to continue his father's legacy and protect his tribe from any harm. He made a vow to himself to never let his people suffer the same fate as his parents.

As he stood over their graves, Khomotso made a promise to his parents that he would use his superpowers to protect his people and ensure that they were never again subjected to such senseless violence. With that, he bid farewell to his parents and left the burial site, determined to fulfil his promise.

Khomotso gathered the survivors and listened to their accounts of the attack. He learned that a Shona tribe had been at odds with Khomotso's people for decades; they had launched a surprise attack under the cover of night. They had been heavily armed with spears and bows, and had set fire to many of the houses in the village.

Khomotso was determined to avenge his parents and protect his people; He devised a plan of attack. He rallied his fellow warriors and together they set out to face the enemy.

Using his superpower of lightning, Khomotso was able to strike the enemy warriors from a distance, Khomotso fought with all his might, his dreadlocks flying in the wind as he launched powerful attacks against the enemy.

The battle was fierce, but Khomotso and his tribe warriors were determined to emerge victorious. They fought for hours, until finally the enemy was defeated and forced to retreat. The survivors of Khomotso's village emerged from their hiding places, cheering and thanking Khomotso and his fellow soldiers for saving them from certain death.

Khomotso, warriors and the villagers helped to rebuild the village, and they became known throughout the land as great warriors and protectors of their people. Though he could never bring back his parents, Khomotso took comfort in knowing that he had avenged their deaths and ensured the safety of his people for generations to come.

King Kgoroshi always knew that Khomotso was a child of prophecy, so he made a decision to appoint him as a lead and chief under him; he knew deep down that one day Khomotso would be his successor; Khomotso had the opportunity to hone his leadership skills and prove himself as a capable and just leader.

However, even as the kingdom thrived, there were always those who sought to undermine Khomotso's authority and challenge his rule. Some were jealous of his success and resented his power, while others sought to take advantage of the kingdom's prosperity for their own gain.

Despite these challenges, Khomotso remained steadfast in his commitment to his people and his kingdom. He continued to make decisions that were in the best interest of all, and he worked tirelessly to ensure that the kingdom remained strong and prosperous.

Over time, Khomotso's reputation as a wise and just leader spread beyond the borders of his kingdom, and he became known throughout the land as a symbol of hope and inspiration.

Chapter 6: First Battle to protect the village

As the sun began to rise over Seshego village, Khomotso was 30 years old when he prepared himself for battle. For he had heard rumours that the neighbouring tribe, the Zulus, were planning to attack his village.

The Zulu tribe, under the leadership of the legendary warrior-king Shaka, was one of the most powerful and feared tribes in all of Africa. Their fierce reputation had spread far and wide, and many neighbouring tribes trembled at the mere mention of their name.

Mashita tribe had long been at odds with the Zulu, with both sides engaging in constant battles and skirmishes over land and resources. Despite their best efforts, however, Khomotso's tribe had never been able to defeat the Zulu in open combat.

King Shaka was a formidable opponent, a true warrior in every sense of the word. He had led his army to countless victories, using his unmatched skill in battle to crush any who dared to stand against him.

But Khomotso knew he was the only one who could defeat Zulu tribe and protect his people. The warrior set out on foot, moving quickly through the tall grasses and trees. He could feel the adrenaline pumping through his veins as he approached the Zulu camp. He could hear the sounds of drums and chanting in the distance, and he knew he was getting closer.

As he approached the camp, he saw the Zulu warriors gathered around a large fire. They were armed with spears and shields, and they looked fierce and ready for battle.

With a burst of supernatural lightning speed, the warrior charged into the camp, knocking over several Zulu warriors in his path. He swung his massive arms, sending several more flying through the air. The Zulu warriors were caught off guard by the warrior's incredible strength and speed, and they struggled to defend themselves.

THE WARRIOR CONTINUED to fight, moving quickly and striking with incredible force. He could feel the power of his supernatural abilities coursing through his body, and he knew he was unstoppable.

As the battle raged on, the warrior began to tire. He had been fighting for hours, and his muscles were starting to ache. But he refused to give up. He knew that his people were counting on him, and he would not let them down.

With one final burst of strength, the warrior charged forward, knocking over several more Zulu warriors. The remaining Zulu warriors looked on in fear as the Khomotso stood victorious.

Khomotso returned to his village, exhausted but triumphant. His people cheered as he entered the village, and they celebrated his victory over the Zulu tribe. From that day forward, Khomotso was known as a hero, a protector of his people, and a symbol of strength and courage.

The battle was a pivotal moment in the warrior's life, as it marks the beginning of his journey to becoming a leader of his people.

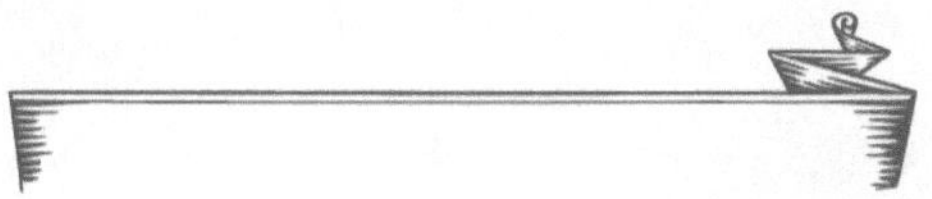

Chapter 7: Rise to Power

On the second day after the fight with Zulu tribe, the warrior stood at the edge of his village, gazing out at the vast before him. He knew that he had a long journey ahead of him, but he was determined to prove himself as a true warrior.

With his supernatural strength and speed, the warrior set out on his journey, traveling from village to village and challenging the strongest warriors of each tribe to battle. He fought with all his might, using his incredible strength to overpower his opponents and his lightning-fast speed to dodge their attacks.

One by one, the warrior defeated the warriors of each tribe, earning their respect and admiration. He became known throughout the land as a fierce and powerful warrior, feared by his enemies and revered by his allies.

As he continued his journey, the warrior encountered Tsonga tribe that was unlike any he had ever seen before. They were fierce and ruthless, with warriors who were powerful because they were using black magic from their witch doctors. But the warrior was not deterred. He knew that he had to defeat this tribe if he was to truly rise to power.

With a fierce determination, the warrior engaged the tribe in battle. The fight was long and gruelling, with both sides taking heavy losses. But in the end, the warrior emerged victorious, using his supernatural strength and speed to overcome his opponents and claim victory.

With this final victory, the warrior had proven himself as the strongest and most powerful warrior in all the land. He had risen to power through his incredible strength and speed, and he would go down in history as one of the greatest warriors of all time.

Chapter 8: Warrior's Growing Reputation

As the Khomotso continued to use his supernatural strength, lightning and speed to defeat his enemies, his reputation began to grow throughout the land. People spoke of him in hushed tones, marvelling at his incredible abilities and the way he seemed to move with lightning-fast speed.

Khomotso was a force to be reckoned with. As a superhero with the power of lightning and super strength, he had faced many foes in battle. But he had a unique fighting skill that set him apart from other superheroes.

Whenever Khomotso engaged in combat, he would first charge his body with lightning, filling himself with energy and power. Then, he would launch himself at his opponent with incredible speed, delivering a series of lightning-fast punches, kicks and using his spear that left his enemies reeling.

However, Khomotso's signature move was his lightning strike. With a flick of his wrist, he could summon a bolt of lightning to strike his enemy, stunning them and leaving them vulnerable to attack. And if he needed to unleash a more devastating attack, he could channel his lightning into a massive bolt that could obliterate anything in its path.

Khomotso's fighting style was as impressive as it was effective. He moved with lightning speed, striking with lightning precision and unleashing bolts of lightning when he needed to. It was a sight to behold, and his enemies trembled at the mere thought of facing him in battle.

Despite his incredible power, Khomotso knew that he couldn't rely solely on his lightning and strength. He was a skilled fighter, trained in various martial arts and combat techniques, and he knew how to use his powers to enhance his already impressive fighting abilities.

Khomotso was a master of hand-to-hand combat, using his lightning-charged fists and kicks to devastating effect. He was also proficient in various weapons, including spears, shields, and bow, which he could imbue with his lightning to make them even deadlier.

But Khomotso's greatest weapon was his mind. He was a strategic thinker, always analysing his opponent's weaknesses and finding ways to exploit them. He could anticipate their moves before they made them, and he always had a plan of attack.

Khomotso's fighting style was a perfect blend of lightning-fast reflexes, superhuman strength, and strategic thinking. He was a true master of combat, feared by his enemies and revered by his allies. And as long as there was evil in the world, he would continue to fight with all his might, using his incredible powers and skills to protect the innocent and defeat his foes.

At first, the warrior was content to simply use his powers to protect his village and those he cared about. But as his reputation grew, he began to realize that he could use his abilities to help others as well.

He travelled from village to village, offering his services to those in need. He fought off bandits and

Wild animals, and even helped to put out a raging fire that threatened to destroy an entire village.

As he travelled, the warrior began to attract followers. People who had heard of his incredible feats of strength and speed began to seek him out, hoping to learn from him and perhaps even gain some of his powers.

At first, the warrior was hesitant to take on disciples. He knew that his powers were not something that could be passed to another, and he didn't want to risk anyone getting hurt by trying to imitate him.

But as he got to know some of the people who sought him out, he began to see that they were sincere in their desire to learn from him. He began to take on a few select students, teaching them the ways of the warrior and helping them to develop their own unique fighting abilities.

As his reputation continued to grow, Khomotso became a legend in his own time. People spoke of him in awe, and many believed that he was a gift from the gods because they didn't know where he got power for he never told a soul how got his powers.

But the warrior remained humble, always remembering that his powers were not his own, but a gift that had been given to him. He continued to use his abilities to help others, and to inspire those around him to be the best that they could be.

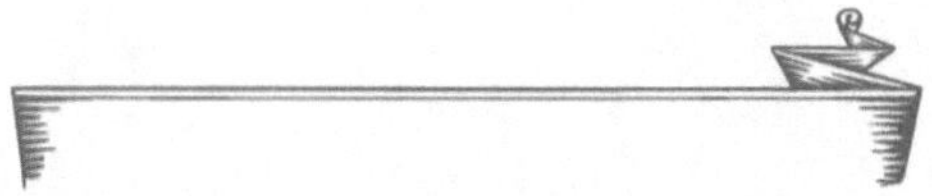

Chapter 9: Growing Influence

As the African warrior continued to travel and help those in need, his influence began to spread beyond the borders of his own land. People from neighbouring countries began to hear of his incredible abilities and the good deeds he had done, and they began to seek him out as well.

At first, the warrior was hesitant to leave his own land and venture into unknown territory. But as he thought about the people who might need his help, he realized that he could not turn his back on them.

So he set out on a journey that would take him far from his home. He travelled through dense forests and across vast deserts, using his supernatural strength and speed to overcome any obstacles that stood in his way.

As he travelled, the warrior encountered many different people and cultures. Some welcomed him with open arms, grateful for his help and guidance. Others were suspicious of him, seeing him as a threat to their own way of life.

But the warrior remained true to his own values and beliefs. He continued to help those in need, regardless of their background or beliefs. And slowly but surely, he began to win over even his most sceptical critics.

As his influence grew, the African warrior began to realize that he had a responsibility to use his powers for the greater good. He began to work with other leaders and warriors, sharing his knowledge and skills with them and helping to create a more peaceful and just world.

And though he faced many challenges and obstacles along the way, the warrior never lost sight of his ultimate goal: to use his supernatural strength and speed to make the world a better place for all.

Chapter 10: Warrior Growing An Army

As the African warrior continued to hone his supernatural strength and speed, he began to attract a following of like-minded individuals who were drawn to his power and charisma. These individuals were also seeking to harness their own fighting combat skills, and the warrior saw an opportunity to build an army of powerful warriors who could help him protect his people and fight against their enemies.

The warrior began to train these individuals in the ways of combat and using spear and shield, teaching them how to fight skilfully with it. He also taught them the importance of discipline and focus, and how to channel their energy in order to achieve their goals.

As the warrior's army grew, so did their reputation. They became known throughout the land as a force to be reckoned with, and their enemies began to fear them. The warrior himself became a legend, with stories of his incredible strength and speed spreading far and wide.

But the warrior knew that he could not rest on his laurels. He continued to train and push himself, always seeking to improve his abilities and those of his army. He also knew that there were still many enemies out there who would seek to harm his people, and he was determined to protect them at all costs.

The warrior and his army continued to fight, He always pushing army to be better and stronger. They faced many challenges and obstacles along the way, but they never gave up. They knew that they were fighting for something greater than themselves, Khomotso's strength and speed was a gift that he had been given in order to protect the weak and make the world a better place.

In the end, the warrior's army became known as one of the greatest forces in all of Africa. They had achieved incredible things together, and had protected their people from countless threats. And the warrior himself had become a legend, a symbol of hope and strength for all who knew him

Chapter 11: War Against Colonizers

As the African warrior continued to hone his supernatural strength and speed, he faced a new challenge. White colonizers had arrived in his country, coming with boats and weapons that the warrior had never seen before. They were determined to take over the land and enslave the people, and the warrior knew that he had to run back to his country fast to protect his people.

The warrior rallied his army and led them into battle against the colonizers. They fought with all their might, using their bows, spears and shields to outmanoeuvre and kill the enemy. The colonizers were taken aback by the ferocity of the warrior and his army, and they soon realized that they were facing a force unlike any they had encountered before.

Despite their superior weapons and technology, the colonizers were no match for the warrior and his army. They were driven back time and time again, and the warrior's legend grew with each victory. The people began to see him as a hero, a symbol of hope and strength in the face of oppression.

BUT THE COLONIZERS were not easily deterred. They continued to send more troops and resources to the country, determined to crush the resistance and take over the land. The warrior knew that he had to come up with a new strategy if he was going to win this war.

He began to use his supernatural abilities in new and creative ways, using his speed to outflank the enemy and his strength to break through their defences. He also began to use his intelligence and strategic thinking to outmanoeuvre the colonizers, setting traps and ambushes that caught them off guard.

As the war raged on, the warrior's legend continued to grow. He became known as a master strategist and a fearless warrior, and his army became known as one of the most formidable forces in all of Africa. And in the end, they emerged victorious.

Chapter 12: Warrior's Epic Battle

For five long years, the warrior and his army fought against the White people. They faced incredible odds, as the colonizers had superior weapons and technology. But the warrior refused to give up. He knew that he was fighting for his people

The battles were brutal and intense, with both sides suffering heavy losses. But the warrior and his army never wavered. They continued to fight with all their might, using their supernatural abilities to outmanoeuvre and outfight the enemy.

As the war raged on, the warrior's legend grew. He became known as a master strategist and a fearless warrior, and his army became known as one of the most formidable forces in all of Africa. And despite the odds against them, they continued to hold their ground and fight for their freedom.

In the end, the warrior and his army emerged victorious. They had driven the colonizers out of the country and secured the freedom of the people. The warrior had become a hero, a symbol of strength and resilience in the face of oppression.

But the victory had come at a great cost. The warrior had lost many of his closest friends and allies in the battles, and he himself had suffered many injuries. He knew that the scars of the war would never fully heal, but he also knew that he had done what was necessary to protect his people.

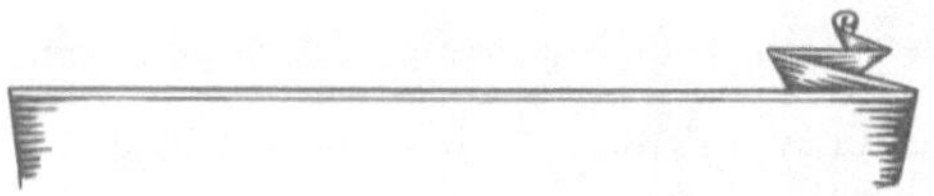

Chapter 13: The Warrior's Victories and Love life

As the African warrior continued to hone his supernatural strength and speed, he found himself facing more and more formidable opponents. But with each battle, he emerged victorious, earning the respect and admiration of his people.

Khomotso rode his horse through the dense jungle, his senses on high alert. He was on a mission to deliver a message to the neighbouring tribe, and he knew that danger lurked around every corner.

As he rode, his thoughts drifted to his childhood girlfriend, Tebogo. They had met years ago, before the war, when they were both young and carefree. He had been drawn to her beauty and her kind heart, and they had fallen in love quickly. Unfortunately, their time together was brief as they were both forced to continue on their journeys, Khomotso promised to find a way to see Tebogo again.

But the war had changed everything. Khomotso had become a warrior, fighting for his people against the white colonizers who sought to take their land and their freedom.

As he emerged from the jungle, he saw the village in the distance. Smoke rose from several huts, and he could hear the sounds of fighting. His heart sank. Had he arrived too late?

He urged his horse forward, sprinting towards the village. As he got closer, he could see that the fighting was fierce. His fellow tribesmen were outnumbered and outgunned, and they were struggling to hold their ground.

Khomotso drew his spear, ready to join the battle, but then he saw her. Tebogo was there, fighting alongside the other women and children. She looked strong and fierce warrior in her own right.

Khomotso's heart swelled with pride and love. He charged forward, cutting down several of the enemy soldiers with ease. Tebogo saw him and smiled, her eyes shining with joy and relief.

They fought together, side by side, as they had so many times before. They moved in perfect unison, their swords flashing in the sunlight. The other tribesmen rallied around them, and soon they had pushed the enemy back.

When the fighting was over, Khomotso and Tebogo embraced, their bodies trembling with adrenaline and emotion. They kissed passionately, forgetting for a moment the war and the danger that surrounded them.

In that moment, they were just two people in love, clinging to each other in the midst of chaos.

As they separated, Khomotso felt a sense of hope. He knew that their love would sustain them through the darkest times, that no matter what the war threw at them, they would face it together.

He looked at Tebogo, his heart full of gratitude and affection. She was his rock, his partner, his soul mate. And he knew that no matter what the future held, they would face it together, hand in hand, with love as their guide.

They fell deeply in love and were married in grant cultural ceremony that was attended by all the tribes in the region.

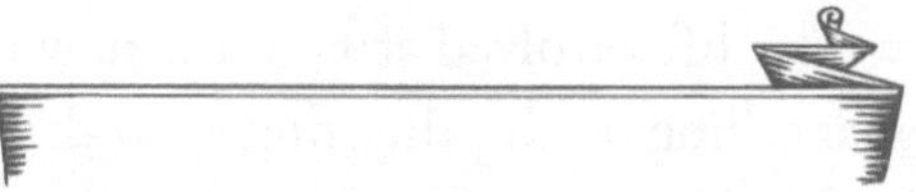

Chapter 14: Birth of Warrior's successors

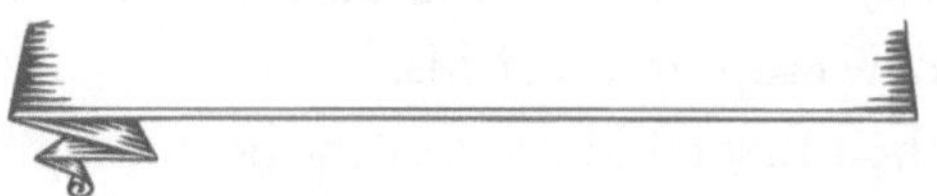

Months had passed since the battle and the ceremony, and life had settled into a semblance of normalcy for Khomotso and Tebogo. They had rebuilt their home, tended to their crops and livestock, and prepared for the coming of their first child.

Tebogo had grown round with the child, her belly swelling with new life. Khomotso was both excited and nervous at the prospect of becoming a father. He had seen so much death and destruction in his life that the idea of creating new life filled him with both hope and fear.

As the weeks passed, Tebogo's due date approached. Khomotso was on edge, unable to sleep or eat properly. He watched his wife's every move, worried that something would go wrong.

Finally, the day arrived. Tebogo went into labor, and Khomotso rushed her to the nearest midwife. He paced the floor, his heart pounding with anxiety, as Tebogo cried out in pain.

Hours passed, and finally, the midwife emerged, holding a small bundle in her arms. Khomotso rushed forward, tears streaming down his face, as he saw his son for the first time.

The baby was perfect, with dark skin and a shock of curly hair. He had his mother's eyes and his father's chin, and Khomotso knew in that moment that he loved him more than anything in the world, They named the child Tumelo(faith).

Tebogo smiled weakly, her eyes shining with tears of joy and exhaustion. She reached out for the baby, cradling him in her arms as she whispered soft words of love and comfort.

For the next few weeks, life revolved around the new baby. Khomotso spent hours holding him, marvelling at the tiny fingers and toes, the soft skin and downy hair.

As the days passed, Tebogo's strength returned, and she began to take charge of the household once more. She cooked meals, tended to the baby, and even found time to plant new crops in the fields.

But the birth of their first child was just the beginning. Tebogo was pregnant again, and this time, they were expecting twins. Khomotso was overjoyed at the news, and he couldn't wait to hold his new babies in his arms.

As the months passed, Tebogo's belly grew round once more. Khomotso watched in awe as his wife carried two lives inside her, her body stretched to its limits.

Finally, the day arrived. Tebogo went into labour once more, and Khomotso rushed her to the midwife's hut.

This time, the birth was harder. Tebogo cried out in pain, her body shaking with the effort of delivering two babies at once. But finally, the midwife emerged, holding two small bundles in her arms. The first twin was a boy and the second one was a girl, They named the first one Kgosi(ruler) and the second one Lerato(Love)

Khomotso rushed forward, tears streaming down his face, as he saw his two children for the first time. They were both perfect, with dark skin and bright eyes. One had a shock of curly hair like his older brother, while the other had straight hair that stood up in tufts.

Khomotso held them both, marvelling at the miracle of their birth. He knew in that moment that his life had been forever changed, that he had been given a gift greater than anything he could ever have imagined.

As the days and weeks passed, Khomotso watched in wonder as his family grew, His children were strong and healthy, with personalities all their own. They ran and played in the fields, their laughter filling the air with joy and happiness.

And through it all, Khomotso knew that he was blessed, because they had two sons and one daughter; the sons inherited their father's supernatural abilities. The daughter, however, was born with a different gift. She had the ability to heal others with just a touch of her hand.

The family lived in peace for many years, but their happiness was not to last. Because neighbouring countries were jealous of the warrior's power and influence, they conspired and launched a surprise attack on his village.

The warrior fought bravely, but he was outnumbered and outmatched. They killed most of his men and they were defeated.

In the end, he was captured and taken prisoner. His wife and children were fled to the nearest country gharatin for their lives, leaving him behind to face an uncertain fate.

But the warrior was not one to give up easily. He used his supernatural strength and speed to break free from his captors and make his way back to his family, 3month after Khomotso raised a new army and trained them, they fought back against the invading countries and emerged victorious once again.

From that day forward, the warrior and warriors were known throughout the land as heroes. They continued to defend their people against all threats, using their supernatural abilities to protect and serve those in need.

And though they faced many challenges along the way, they never lost sight of what was truly important: their love for each other and their commitment to their people.

Chapter 15: Training the Next Generation

Khomotso knew that his children were special from the moment they were born. As they grew, he saw that they possessed the same superpowers that he did - strength, lightning, speed and healing. But he also knew that these powers could be dangerous if not controlled.

So he began to train his children, teaching them how to harness their abilities and use them for good. He started with the basics, teaching them how to focus their energy and channel it into their limbs.

His eldest son, Tumelo, was a natural fighter. He had inherited his father's strength and speed, and Khomotso knew that he would be a powerful warrior one day. But Tumelo was impulsive, and Khomotso worried that he would use his powers without thinking.

So Khomotso began to teach Tumelo control. He showed him how to breathe deeply and focus his energy, how to move with grace and precision. They practiced every day, running through the fields and lifting boulders with ease.

Khomotso's daughter, Lerato, had inherited unique healing powers. But she was also sensitive and emotional, and Khomotso worried that she would be overwhelmed by her abilities.

So he began to teach Lerato how to control her emotions. He showed her how to breathe deeply and clear her mind, how to focus her energy and channel it into her fingertips. They practiced every day, zapping targets with lightning bolts and learning how to deflect incoming attacks.

His youngest son, Kgosi, had inherited his father's speed. But he was also mischievous and easily distracted, and Khomotso worried that he would use his powers for pranks and jokes.

So he began to teach Kgosi discipline. He showed him how to focus his energy and control his movements, how to run with precision and avoid obstacles. They practiced every day, running laps around the village and dodging through crowds of people.

As the years passed, Khomotso watched his children grow stronger and more skilled. They became a team, working together to protect their village from harm. They ran through the fields and leaped over fences, their powers combining to create a force to be reckoned with.

And through it all, Khomotso knew that he had done his duty as a father and a warrior. He had trained the next generation, preparing them for the battles that lay ahead. He knew that his children would carry on his legacy, fighting for justice and defending their people with all their might.

Chapter 16: New Strategy

Khomotso had been fighting against the white colonizers for many years, and he knew that their tactics were changing. They were becoming more organized, more ruthless, and more determined to take over African land.

Khomotso had always been a fierce warrior, but he knew that brute force alone would not be enough to defeat the colonizers. He needed a new strategy, one that would allow him to outmanoeuvre and outsmart his enemies.

So he gathered his trusted advisors and began to brainstorm. They talked for hours, debating different ideas and weighing the risks and benefits of each one. They knew that the stakes were high, and that one wrong move could mean the end of their people's freedom.

After much discussion, they came up with a plan. They would create a network of spies, gathering information on the colonizers' movements and plans. They would also begin to sabotage their supply chains, disrupting their ability to move troops and resources.

Khomotso knew that this plan would require patience and careful execution. He would need to choose his spies wisely, and ensure that they were loyal to their cause. He would also need to train them in the art of espionage, teaching them how to blend in with the colonizers and gather information without being detected.

As he began to put his plan into action, Khomotso realized that he needed more resources. He needed weapons, food, and supplies to sustain his people and carry out his mission. So he sent a message to neighbouring tribes, asking for their support.

To his relief, the response was positive. The other tribes agreed to join forces with Khomotso and help him in his fight against the colonizers. They sent supplies and warriors, eager to join in the battle for freedom.

Khomotso knew that this was a turning point in the war. With the support of other tribes and his new network of spies, he felt confident that they could gain the upper hand.

But he also knew that the colonizers would not give up easily. They were determined to take over African land, and they would stop at nothing to achieve their goal.

So Khomotso and his warriors continued to train, honing their skills and preparing for the battles to come. They practiced their new strategy, gathering information and sabotaging supply chains. They also continued to use their superpowers, combining their strength, lightning, and speed to overwhelm their enemies.

As the war raged on, Khomotso's new strategy proved to be effective. They were able to gain valuable information about the colonizers' plans, and they were able to disrupt their supply chains, causing chaos and confusion.

But the war was far from over. The colonizers continued to fight back, using their superior technology and resources to push back against Khomotso's forces.

Khomotso knew that he would need to continue to adapt and evolve his strategy if they were to succeed in their fight for freedom.

He would need to stay one step ahead of his enemies, using every tool at his disposal to outmanoeuvre and outsmart them.

And so, Khomotso and his warriors continued to fight for their people and their land. They knew that the battle would be long and difficult, but they were determined to fight until the end.

Chapter 17: Uniting the Tribes

Khomotso and his children had always understood the importance of unity among the tribes. They knew that only by working together could they hope to defeat the colonizers and reclaim their land.

As they traveled across the land, they met with leaders from different tribes. They listened to their concerns and shared their own stories of struggle and resistance. They learned about each tribe's unique strengths and challenges, and they discussed ways to work together towards a common goal.

One of the first tribes they met with was the Zulu tribe, led by King Shaka. The Zulu were known for their fierce warriors and their highly organized tactics. Khomotso and his children were impressed by the Zulu's discipline and strength, and they recognized the potential for a powerful alliance.

For many years, their respective nations had been in constant conflict, with both sides engaging in battles and raids against each other.

However, the arrival of European colonizers changed everything. Khomotso and King Shaka both realized that the real threat to their people's independence and sovereignty was not each other, but the foreign invaders who sought to exploit and subjugate their lands.

One day, Khomotso decided to reach out to King Shaka to propose a truce and a joint effort to push back against the colonizers. Despite their differences and the history of animosity between their tribes, Khomotso believed that they could put aside their past grievances for the sake of their shared future.

At first, King Shaka was sceptical of Khomotso's proposal. He had been raised to believe that the Pedi people were his enemies, and he struggled to overcome his ingrained prejudices. However, Khomotso was persistent and persuasive, using his gift of storytelling to weave a compelling narrative of a united Africa, free from the yoke of foreign domination.

Gradually, King Shaka began to see the wisdom of Khomotso's argument. He recognized that the Europeans posed a grave threat not just to the Zulu kingdom, but to all the peoples of Africa. He also realized that Khomotso was not just a skilled storyteller and super human, but a wise and honourable leader who shared his commitment to protecting their people's autonomy.

NEXT, THEY TRAVELED to the Tsonga tribe, led by Dzanani Dyondzani. The Tsonga were known for their skilled hunters and their deep knowledge of the land. Khomotso and his children spent time with the hunters, learning their techniques and gaining their trust. They saw how the Tsonga's knowledge of the land could be a valuable asset in the fight against the colonizers.

They also met with the Ndebele tribe, led by Bhekithemba Siyabonga. The Ndebele were known for their beautiful artwork and their rich cultural traditions. Khomotso and his children were fascinated by the Ndebele's unique style, and they recognized the value of cultural exchange and collaboration.

In their travels, they also met with the Venda tribe, led by Dakalo Radzhelani. The Venda were known for their deep spiritual connection to the land and their strong sense of community. Khomotso and his children were inspired by the Venda's sense of unity and cooperation, and they recognized the potential for a powerful coalition.

Finally, they travelled to the Xhosa tribe, led by Khwezi Qaqambile, and the Swati tribe, led by Simphiwe Sifiso. The Xhosa were known for their skilled craftsmen and their powerful spiritual beliefs, while the Swati were known for their skilled warriors and their deep connection to their ancestors. Khomotso and his children recognized the unique strengths of each tribe, and they saw how these strengths could be used to build a more powerful and united front against the colonizers.

With each tribe they met, Khomotso and his children worked to build trust and understanding. They shared their own stories and struggles, and they listened to the stories of others. They recognized the importance of cultural exchange and collaboration, and they began to see how each tribe's unique strengths could be used to build a more powerful and united front.

Over time, the coalition of tribes grew stronger and more united. They shared resources and information, and they coordinated their attacks against the colonizers. They recognized the power of their diversity and their shared history of resistance, and they worked together towards a common goal.

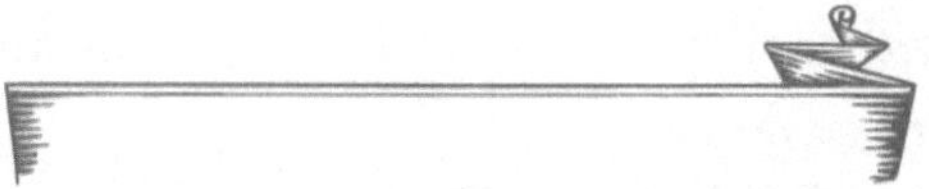

Chapter 18: The Arrival of the Colonizers

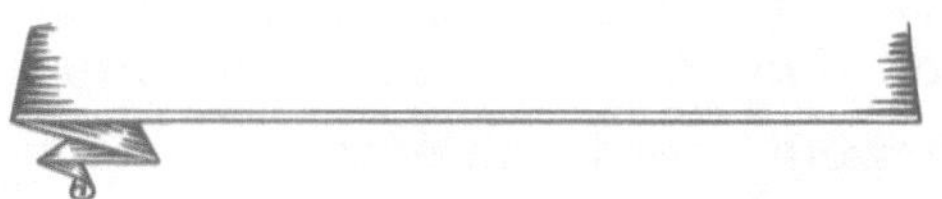

One day, as Khomotso and his children were patrolling the coast, they saw something on the horizon. At first, it was just a speck in the distance, but as it grew closer, they could see that it was a massive ship, its sails billowing in the wind.

Khomotso signalled to his children to be on high alert, and they quickly took up positions along the coast. They watched in disbelief as the ship approached, a large board emblazoned with the colours of the colonizers flying high above it.

As the ship came closer, they could see that it was heavily armed, with cannons lining its sides and rows of musket-wielding soldiers standing on deck. Khomotso and his children knew that this was not a friendly visit, and they braced themselves for whatever was to come.

The ship anchored just off the coast, and a small boat was lowered into the water. Several men in unfamiliar clothing rowed towards the shore, their faces twisted into sneers. As they reached the shore, they jumped out of the boat and onto the sand, their muskets at the ready.

Khomotso stepped forward, his muscles tense and his senses heightened. He could see the hatred and greed in the colonizers' eyes, and he knew that they were not here to make peace.

Khomotso asked "What do you want?" he demanded, his voice steady and strong.

One of the white colonizers stepped forward, a sneer on his face. "We have come to claim this land for our own," he said. "We have been sent by our king to establish a colony here, and we will stop at nothing to make it a success."

Khomotso felt a surge of anger rise within him. This land had been his people's home for generations, and he would not let the colonizers take it away from them. He knew that they would need to be strong and united if they were to resist the colonizers' advance.

He signalled to his children, who had been waiting just behind him. "We must unite the tribes," he said. "Only together can we hope to resist the colonizers' advance."

His children nodded in agreement, their eyes burning with determination. They knew that this would not be an easy fight, but they were ready to do whatever it took to protect their land and their people.

As the colonizers began to establish their presence on the land, Khomotso and his children worked tirelessly to unite the tribes. They traveled across the land, sharing their stories of struggle and resistance, and building trust and understanding among the different tribes.

Over time, the coalition of tribes grew stronger and more united. They shared resources and information, and they coordinated their attacks against the colonizers. They recognized the power of their diversity and their shared history of resistance, and they worked together towards a common goal.

This was the moment they had been dreading, the warrior Khomotso had been fighting against the white colonizers for years, and he knew that their tactics were changing. He had heard stories of how the white colonizers had taken over other parts of Africa, enslaving the people and stealing their land. They knew that they could not allow the same thing to happen to their own people.

As the colonizers began to set up camp on the shore, Khomotso and his children gathered their people. They knew that they needed to act fast, before the colonizers could gain a foothold in their land.

Chapter 19: The Great Warfare

Colonizer started preparing for the fight, determined to take over the land and enslave the people. Khomotso and his sons knew that they could not defeat the colonizers alone, so they rallied their own tribe, as well as the neighbouring tribes, to join them in battle.

The battle lasted for two long weeks, with both sides suffering heavy losses. The colonizers were well-armed and well-trained, but Khomotso and his sons were able to use their superpowers to turn the tide of the battle in their favour.

Tumelo and Kgosi were ready to fight alongside their father, each using their own unique powers to devastating effect. Kgosi had inherited Khomotso's lightning powers; the elder son Tumelo had the strength of ten men. Together, they were an unstoppable force, able to take on multiple enemies at once.

The neighbouring tribes, led by their respective leaders, fought with a fierce determination. The Zulu tribe, led by Shaka Zulu, was particularly effective, with their well-trained warriors and expert tactics. The Tsonga tribe, led

BY DZANANI DYONDZANI, provided invaluable support with their knowledge of the land and their ability to navigate the dense forests and swamps.

The Ndebele tribe, led by Bhekithemba Siyabonga, provided crucial backup, using their knowledge of siege warfare to help lay siege to the colonizer's stronghold. The Venda tribe, led by Dakalo Radzhelani, provided much-needed supplies and food, ensuring that the warriors had the energy to continue fighting.

The Xhosa tribe, led by Khwezi Qaqambile, used their expert knowledge of the enemy to devise effective battle strategies, while the Swati tribe, led by Simphiwe Sifiso, provided valuable intelligence and reconnaissance.

Despite the heavy losses on both sides, Khomotso and his allies emerged victorious. The colonizers were forced to retreat, their pride and arrogance shattered by the strength and determination of the African warriors.

Khomotso and his sons were hailed as heroes, their names spoken with reverence by their people and the neighbouring tribes. They had united the tribes in a common cause, proving that even in the face of

Overwhelming odds, the power of unity and determination could triumph over even the most formidable of foes.

The battle had been long and hard, but it had also been a turning point in the history of the African continent. It had shown that the people of Africa were not to be underestimated, and that they would fight with everything they had to defend their land and their people.

As the dust settled and the wounded were tended to, Khomotso and his sons stood on the battlefield, looking out at the land they had fought so hard to protect. They knew that the fight was far from over, and that there would always be those who would seek to take what was not theirs.

But they were ready, and they would never back down. For they were warriors, with superpowers beyond those of ordinary men, and they were willing to do whatever, it took to defend their land and their people.

Khomotso and his sons emerged victorious after two weeks of gruelling warfare against the white colonizers and their army. The neighbouring tribes who had allied with Khomotso and his tribe were also in a joyous mood, As they have fought with bravery and valence to protect their land and people.

The day after the battle, Khomotso and his sons were hailed as heroes and were celebrated throughout the land. The victory celebration took place in the main village square, where the elders of the tribe had prepared a feast in honour of the brave warriors.

Khomotso stood tall and proud at the centre, His sons, who had fought alongside him, stood on either side, equally proud of their accomplishments, with his hair in long dreadlocks that hung down to his shoulders, adding to his impressive stature. On his forehead, there was a god's prophetic mark, a sign of his heritage and a symbol of his authority among his people.

When Khomotso was adorned in his ceremonial garb, he was truly a sight to behold. He had worn in gold and jewellery, including a shining golden belt and bracelets on his wrists. A chain of glittering gold adorned his neck, drawing attention to his piercing, golden eyes.

IN HIS LEFT HAND, HE held a spear, a weapon that he was skilled at wielding. The spear was not only a tool of war but also a symbol of his power and authority.

As the celebration continued, Khomotso addressed the crowd, thanking them for their unwavering support and for standing by him and his family during the battle. He spoke of the great sacrifice his people had made, and how their bravery had resulted in a victory that would never be forgotten.

The neighbouring tribe leaders, who had joined forces with Khomotso's tribe, were also present at the celebration. They too spoke of the strength and courage of the warriors, and how the victory would be remembered for generations to come.

As the night wore on the celebration continued with music and dancing. The sounds of drums and singing filled the air, and the people danced around a large bonfire in the centre of the square.

Khomotso's wife, Tebogo, and their children, who had also played a crucial role in the victory, were present at the celebration. Khomotso took his wife's hand and led her to the centre of the square, where they danced together under the moonlit sky. Their children watched on, filled with joy and pride for their parents and the tribe.

The feast continued throughout the night, with food and drink flowing freely. The people of the tribe were grateful for the victory, but they were also mindful that the battle was not over. They knew that the white colonizers would return, and they needed to be prepared.

Khomotso, his sons, and the neighbouring tribe leaders discussed plans for the future. They knew that they needed to unite all the tribes in the land, to stand together and fight against the common enemy.

As the night drew to a close, the people of the tribe retired to their homes, filled with a sense of hope and determination. They knew that their victory was just the beginning, and that they had a long and difficult road ahead. But they were ready to face whatever challenges came their way, united in their goal to protect their land and their people.

But their greatest challenge came in the form of a powerful witch, who had taken over a nearby kingdom and was enslaving its people. Khomotso and Tebogo knew they had to act fast to stop her.

WITH THEIR WEAPONS at the ready - spears, bows, and shields - Khomotso and Tebogo charged into battle against the witch's minions. Khomotso's lightning strikes and super strength powers were unmatched, while Tebogo's combat skills proved invaluable in close quarters combat.

Despite their bravery and skill, the witch proved to be a formidable opponent. She unleashed dark magic that sent waves of darkness through the air, threatening to swallow up Khomotso and Tebogo. But the two warriors stood their ground, determined to protect the innocent and defeat the witch once and for all.

Finally, after hours of a long and gruelling battle, Khomotso and Tebogo emerged victorious. The witch was defeated, and banished from the kingdom; it was then freed from her tyrannical grip.

From that day on, Khomotso and Tebogo continued to fight for justice and protect their people from any threat that came their way. They became legends in their own time, and their story was told throughout the land for generations to come.

The witch was banished to the outskirts of the kingdom years ago, after she had attempted to take over the throne.

However, the witch had not given up on her quest for power. She had spent 3 years honing her dark magic and building an army of ugly minions and zombies, waiting for the perfect opportunity to strike.

When Khomotso and Tebogo had heard of the witch's reign of terror, they knew that they had to act fast. They gathered tribal warriors and marched towards the witch's kingdom

As they approached the kingdom, Khomotso and Tebogo could feel the dark magic emanating from the witch's underground castle. The air was thick with an ominous energy, and the sky was shrouded in a deep, unnatural darkness.

As they entered the underground door gates, Khomotso and Tebogo were met by the witch's ugly minions, who swarmed towards them with deadly intent. Khomotso's lightning strikes and super strength powers were unmatched, and he fought with all his might against the relentless onslaught of the witch's minions.

Meanwhile, Tebogo engaged in close quarters combat, wielding her spear with deadly precision and using her combat skills to dodge and weave through the throng of enemies.

The battle raged on for hours, with neither side able to gain the upper hand. But the witch's power was too great, and she eventually emerged from one of her underground room to face Khomotso and Tebogo herself.

The witch's power was immense, and she unleashed a barrage of dark magic that sent shockwaves through the air. But Khomotso and Tebogo stood firm, using their weapons and combat skills to fend off the witch's attacks.

Finally, after a long and gruelling battle, Khomotso and Tebogo managed to overpower the witch. They used their combined strength and Khomotso's superpowers to break her spell and free her people from her tyranny.

The witch was captured and burned alive, they returned to their own village, ready to face whatever new challenges lay ahead, knowing that they would always be ready to fight for what was right.

Chapter 20: The Warrior appointed to be a King

As the African warrior continued to hone his supernatural strength and speed, his fame began to spread far and wide. People from all over the world came to witness his incredible abilities, and he quickly became known as one of the most powerful warriors in history.

But the warrior's fame was not limited to his own abilities. He had also fathered two sons and one daughter; the sons had inherited his incredible powers. Together, the three of them became an unstoppable force, feared and respected by all who knew of them.

As the years went by, the warrior's sons grew into powerful young men, each with their own unique strengths and abilities. They trained tirelessly with their father, honing their skills and preparing for the day when they would take their place as leaders of their people.

After King Kgoroshi's death, the kingdom was thrown into a state of mourning. But amidst the grief, there was also a sense of anticipation, as everyone wondered who would take up the mantle of leadership. To the surprise of many, King Kgoroshi's successor was not one of his own children, but Khomotso, a trusted advisor and military leader who had served the kingdom for decades.

Despite initial doubts and concerns from some of the advisors and leaders, Khomotso proved himself to be a capable and wise king. He had a deep understanding of the needs of his people and was able to make sound decisions that were both profitable and beneficial for the kingdom. His years of experience leading the army also made him a formidable opponent to any enemies who sought to challenge the kingdom's sovereignty.

As Khomotso settled into his new role, he did so with grace and humility, acknowledging the legacy of his predecessor and working hard to earn the respect and trust of his subjects. He also made a point of fostering strong relationships with neighbouring kingdoms, believing that a united front was essential to ensuring peace and prosperity for all.

Over time, Khomotso proved himself to be a worthy successor to King Kgoroshi. Under his leadership, the kingdom prospered and thrived, with his reign remembered as a time of stability and progress. And while his appointment as king may have been unexpected, it was a decision that ultimately proved to be the right one for the kingdom and its people.

Most trusted advisors, Motlalepule and Kwena. They had been with him since he was a young warrior and had proven their loyalty and bravery time and time again. As they walked through the village, the people cheered and bowed before him he was then to be appointed by his people to be their king.

Khomotso's appointment ceremony was a grand affair, bringing together all the tribes and nations of the kingdom to witness the passing of the torch to a new King. The ceremony was held in a large open field, with rows of decorated chairs and benches set up for the dignitaries and guests.

As the sun rose on the day of the ceremony, the air was filled with the sound of drumming and singing, as the people of the kingdom came together to celebrate the new king's ascension to the throne. Khomotso appeared dressed in his finest ceremonial garb, resplendent in his golden jewellery and holding his spear.

The ceremony began with a procession of dancers and musicians, who moved gracefully through the crowd, drawing everyone's attention to the centre of the field where Khomotso stood. There, he was greeted by the leaders of the various tribes and nations who pledged their allegiance to him, promising to support him in his rule and protect the kingdom against all threats.

After the formal pledges were made, the elders of the kingdom stepped forward to present Khomotso with the symbols of his authority - a ceremonial staff, a crown of feathers and animal skins, and a royal robe. As each item was presented to him, a cheer went up from the crowd, signalling their approval of the new king.

Khomotso then took his place on the throne, simple wooden chairs that had been carved with intricate patterns and adorned with colourful feathers animal skins. As he sat down, the elders knelt before him, offering their prayers and blessings for his reign.

The ceremony ended with a great feast, where the people of the kingdom gathered to celebrate the new king and his reign. The air was filled with the sounds of laughter and cultural music, as everyone toasted to a bright future under the leadership of their new king, Khomotso.

But with the crown came new responsibilities and challenges. The neighbouring tribe, led by a powerful sorcerer named Arhaan Vedant, had been raiding their nearest neighbour country for months. King Khomotso fought with all his might to protect his people.

Arhaan Vedant, sorcerer supreme who's from India appeared in Khomotso's kingdom, leading an army of strange creatures and wielding dark magic. The sorcerer, known as the Supreme Leader, was determined to conquer the land and enslave its people.

The Supreme Leader, the sorcerer who challenged Khomotso and his army, was a tall and imposing figure, with a regal bearing and an air of menace about him. He was dressed in flowing robes of deep crimson and gold, with intricate patterns embroidered along the hem.

His skin was dark and smooth, and his eyes glittered with an otherworldly light. He wore a golden circlet around his forehead, studded with glittering gems that sparkled in the sunlight.

In one hand, he held a sceptre of polished ebony, carved with arcane symbols and encrusted with jewels. With a wave of this sceptre, he could summon creatures from other dimensions, or unleash bolts of dark energy that could obliterate his enemies.

His voice was deep and commanding, resonating with power and authority. When he spoke, his words carried an aura of dark magic, causing those who heard them to feel a chill run down their spine.

Despite his imposing appearance, however, Khomotso was not intimidated. He knew that the sorcerer's power was great, but he was confident in his own abilities, and in the strength of his army. He knew that together, they could overcome any obstacle, no matter how great the challenge.

Khomotso knew that he had to act quickly to stop the Supreme Leader and his army. He called upon his two sons, who were both brave and skilled warriors in their own right, to join him in battle.

As they prepared for the fight, Khomotso's lightning powers crackled and sparked around him, energizing his body and sharpening his senses. The Supreme

Leader's army appeared on the horizon, and Khomotso and his sons charged forward to meet them.

The battle was fierce and intense, with the Supreme Leader's army using dark magic to summon creatures from other dimensions to fight for them. But Khomotso and his sons were relentless, fighting with all their might and using their supernatural powers to gain the upper hand.

As the battle raged on, the Supreme Leader himself appeared, teleporting from place to place and launching deadly spells at Khomotso and his army. But Khomotso was too quick for him, dodging the sorcerer's attacks and countering with lightning strikes and powerful blows.

He used his supernatural strength and speed, honed through years of training and battles, and led his army and sons into battle.

In the end, Khomotso emerged victorious, using his lightning powers to strike down the Supreme Leader and his army. The people of the kingdom rejoiced, celebrating their hero and his sons for their bravery and strength.

But the sorcerer was not so easily defeated. He had one last trick up his sleeve - a powerful curse that would bring darkness and destruction to the village. King Khomotso killed the sorcerer by cutting his head off but unfortunately the spell was cast already.

He called upon his advisors, Motlalepule; Kwena together with his sons helped him find a way to break the curse. They searched high and low, consulting with the village elders and the spirits of their ancestors. Finally, they found the solution - a rare herb that could counteract the curse.

The African warrior set out on a dangerous journey to find the herb, using his supernatural speed to outrun any danger that came his way. He faced many obstacles, including treacherous terrain and dangerous animals, but he never gave up.

Finally, he found the herb and brought it back to the village. With the help of the village elders, he performed a powerful ritual that broke the curse and brought light back to the village.

The new king had proven himself to be a true leader, using his supernatural strength and speed to protect his people and overcome any obstacle in his path. He knew that there would be more challenges to come, but he was ready to face them with the same determination and bravery that had brought him this far.

Chapter 21: The Khomotso's Final Battle

King Khomotso was 76 year old his superpower were starting to be weak, he couldn't run and move as fast as he did when was young. Other Kings from different nations heard it and saw it as an opportunity to kill him. Khomotso was now an old man, and his once powerful body was now frail and weak. His superpowers were starting to wane, and he was no longer able to move as fast or fight as fiercely as he once did. However, he was still the king of the Mashita tribe, and he took his duties as seriously as he had always done.

One day, news reached Khomotso that several kings from other countries had gathered together with the intention of attacking him and taking over his lands. Khomotso knew that his weakened state would make it difficult for him to defend his people against such a formidable enemy, but he was determined to protect his tribe at any cost.

He called his two sons, who were now fully grown and had become powerful warriors in their own right. He told them of the impending attack and asked for their help in defending the tribe. They agreed without hesitation and began to prepare for war.

KHOMOTSO KNEW THAT he needed more than just his own tribe to fight off this new threat. He sent out messengers to neighbouring tribes, asking for their aid in defending against the attack. Some were hesitant, but others answered the call, and soon a powerful army had been assembled.

Khomotso, his sons, and the assembled army marched out to meet the invading forces. The two sides clashed on the battlefield, and the fight was fierce and brutal. Khomotso's powers may have weakened, but his experience and skill in battle were still sharp.

With his two sons by his side, Khomotso fought valiantly against the invading forces. Lightning bolts flew from his fingertips, and his powerful blows sent his enemies flying. His sons used their own superpowers to devastating effect, striking down their enemies with incredible speed and strength.

The battle raged on for two days, with neither side gaining a clear advantage. But in the end, it was Khomotso and his army that emerged victorious. The enemy forces were driven back, and the invading kings were victorious.

FINALLY, AFTER DAYS and hours of fighting, the King emerged victorious. His enemies lay defeated on the battlefield, and his army cheered in triumph. Tumelo and Kgosi proved themselves to be true warriors by using their powers to protect the land and people.

But the victory was bittersweet. The King knew that this would be his final battle, and that he would soon pass on his crown to one of his sons as a successor. He had fought many battles in his lifetime, but this one had been the most epic of them all.

As he looked out over the battlefield, the King knew that his legacy would live on. His people would remember him as a great warrior, a true leader, and a protector of their land. And he knew that his first born would carry on his legacy, using his own supernatural powers to protect their people and defeat their enemies.

And that day came sooner than anyone had expected. The warrior King was now an old man who lived 109 years, but he always knew that his time was coming to an end. He called his sons to him and told them that it was time for them to take their place as protectors of the land.

The two young men were hesitant at first, unsure if they were ready for such a great responsibility. But their father had faith in them, and he knew that they would make great leaders.

Chapter 22: The Warrior's Departure

Khomotso and Tebogo had lived a long and fulfilled life together, but all good things must come to an end. They were both very old and their time on this earth was coming to a close. It was a quiet evening in the village when Khomotso felt a sudden pain in his chest. He knew his time had come, and he called for his family to come to his side.

Tebogo, who had been resting in another room, heard the commotion and rushed to Khomotso's side. She knew what was happening, and the look in Khomotso's eyes confirmed it. They shared a knowing look, and Tebogo held Khomotso's hand tightly.

Their children and grandchildren surrounded them, offering their love and support during this difficult time. Khomotso's breathing became laboured and his grip on Tebogo's hand began to weaken. She leaned in close to him and whispered, "its okay, my love. We will be together again soon."

Khomotso took his last breath and closed his eyes. His body went limp, and Tebogo could feel his spirit leaving him. She looked up at their family, tears streaming down her face, and said, "He's gone."

The family mourned the loss of their beloved Khomotso, but they knew he was now a god, watching over them from above. They held a grand funeral procession for him, honouring his life and the legacy he had left behind.

However, Tebogo's health began to decline rapidly after Khomotso's passing. She had always been strong, but the loss of her beloved had taken a toll on her. She passed away peacefully in her sleep a few months later, surrounded by her family.

The entire village mourned the loss of their great leaders, but they found comfort in knowing that Khomotso and Tebogo were now together again, as gods, looking over them and guiding them.

The night of their passing was marked by a grand celebration, with fires burning bright and drums beating loudly. The people of the village believed that Khomotso and Tebogo had ascended to the heavens and become gods, watching over them and guiding them from above.

The stars in the sky twinkled brightly that night, and the villagers believed that each star represented a loved one who had passed on to become a god. Khomotso and Tebogo's stars shone the brightest, a testament to their great deeds and the love they had shared.

As the celebration came to an end, the villagers knew that life would never be the same without Khomotso. However, they also knew that their legacy would live on, and that their gods would always be with them, guiding them through the ups and downs of life.

And so it was that the warrior's first son took his place as a king, ruling over their people with wisdom and strength. They continued to train and hone their abilities, always striving to be the best they could be.

And though their father had passed on, his legacy lived on through them. They were the living embodiment of his incredible strength and speed, and they used their powers to protect their people and ensure that their legacy would never be forgotten.

Chapter 23: After the death of warrior

Years passed after the death of the great King and warrior Khomotso, his children had grown into powerful leaders in their own right. Tumelo, the eldest son, had taken over as king and had continued his father's legacy of protecting their nation with his supernatural abilities. His younger brother, Kgosi, had become a skilled warrior and had taken on the role of leading the army. Their sister, Lerato, had become a wise and respected advisor to the king and a healer the nation.

2years after the death of Khomotso, Tumelo, the older brother, was reigning with integrity and loyalty towards his people. He was wise, just, and loved by all in the kingdom. He led with strength, courage, and fairness, and his rule was prosperous for all. However, his younger brother, Kgosi, was hateful and envious. He felt that the throne should have been his, and that he was more deserving of it than his brother.

As time passed, Kgosi's envy and jealousy grew more and more intense. He plotted to overthrow Tumelo and take the throne for himself. He gathered a group of loyal followers,

And they began to make plans to take over the kingdom. They knew that they could not defeat Tumelo in a fair fight, so they decided to use treachery instead.

One night, while Tumelo was sleeping peacefully in his bed, Kgosi and his men crept into his room. They drew their weapons and attacked him, catching him off guard. Tumelo fought back as best he could, but he was outnumbered and outmatched. He was struck down, and Kgosi declared himself as the new king.

Lerato, Tumelo's younger sister, was horrified by what had happened. She had always been close to her older brother, and she knew that Kgosi was not fit to rule. But Kgosi had other plans for her. He forced her to swear loyalty to him and his rule, threatening her with violence if she did not comply.

Despite his victory, Kgosi knew that he had made a grave mistake. He had killed his own brother, and he had taken the throne through treachery and deceit. He knew that his rule would always be tainted by his actions, and that he would never truly be respected or loved by his people.

As Kgosi sat on the throne, he began to realize the true cost of his ambition. He had lost the love of his sister, the respect of his people, and the trust of those who had once followed him. He knew that he would never be able to live up to his brother's legacy, and that he would always be haunted by the memory of what he had done.

Chapter 24: The Rise of Lerato

After the death of Tumelo, the rightful heir to the throne, Khomotso's youngest daughter Lerato was forced to align with her treacherous brother Kgosi. She was torn between her loyalty to her family and her duty to her people.

Kgosi, now the king, was ruling with an iron fist, and his people lived in fear of his wrath. He was a paranoid ruler, constantly looking over his shoulder and suspicious of everyone around him. Lerato saw the suffering of her people and knew she had to do something.

One day, Lerato snuck out of the palace and disguised herself as a commoner to explore the streets of her kingdom. She was horrified by what she saw. The streets were dirty, the people were starving, and the once-thriving markets were now empty.

Lerato knew she had to act fast. She returned to the palace and began secretly meeting with the other members of the royal council, hoping to gain their support. She shared her plan to overthrow Kgosi and restore the kingdom to its former glory. The council was hesitant at first, fearing the repercussions of defying the king. But Lerato's passion and determination won them over. They began to devise a plan to overthrow Kgosi and put Lerato on the throne.

The plan was risky and dangerous, but Lerato knew it was the only way to save her people. They would need to gather a large army and launch a surprise attack on the palace.

Lerato and her allies spent months planning and preparing for the attack. They gathered their forces from neighbouring kingdoms and trained rigorously for battle.

The day of the attack arrived, and Lerato led her army into battle. The palace was heavily guarded, but they were able to break through and take control. Kgosi was captured and brought before Lerato, who was now the new queen.

Lerato could feel the weight of her newfound power, but she knew she had to use it for good. She began to implement policies to help the people and restore the kingdom to its former glory.

Lerato became known as the benevolent queen who brought peace and prosperity to her people. She had finally fulfilled her duty as a member of the royal family and as a leader of her people.

Chapter 25: Khomotso's daughter Lerato takes over

As the years went by, Lerato proved to be a capable leader despite the difficult circumstances that surrounded her. Her father Khomotso had instilled in her the same values he held dear - strength, courage, and compassion for her people. Under her leadership, the Mashita tribe prospered and continued to grow stronger.

Despite her many successes, Lerato always felt a sense of loneliness. She longed for someone to share her life with, someone who understood the weight of her responsibilities and the importance of her tribe. And then, one day, she met him.

He was an older warrior who had fought alongside her father since the very beginning. His name was Motlalepula, and he was wise and strong, with a deep sense of loyalty to the Mashita tribe. When he and Lerato met, there was an instant connection between them. They talked for hours, and she was struck by his kindness and his gentle nature.

As they spent more time together, Lerato and Motlalepula fell in love. They were from different generations, but their bond was strong and unbreakable. Lerato knew that her people would not approve of her marrying an older man, but she didn't care. She loved him, and that was all that mattered.

After a year of courtship, Lerato and Motlalepula were married in a simple ceremony attended by their closest friends and family. The Mashita tribe was overjoyed to see their leader so happy, and they welcomed Motlalepula with open arms.

For the next few years, Lerato and Motlalepula lived a peaceful life together, ruling over the Mashita tribe and raising their son, Letago. But as Letago grew older, Lerato began to notice something strange about him. He had unique superpower.

At first, Lerato was scared. She remembered the pain and suffering that had come with her father's abilities, and she didn't want her son to suffer the same fate. But Motlalepula reassured her, telling her that Letago was strong and could handle anything that came his way.

As Letago grew stronger in his abilities, Lerato began to see the potential for greatness in him. She knew that he could be the one to lead the Mashita tribe into a new era, one where they were even stronger and more prosperous than before.

But as Lerato began to make plans for Letago's future, she realized that there were those who didn't want to see him succeed. Her younger brother Kgosi, who had taken the throne by force, saw Letago as a threat to his own power. He began to make plans to eliminate him, just as he had done to their older brother Tumelo years before.

Lerato knew that she had to protect her son at all costs. She began to train him in secret, teaching him how to harness his powers and use them for good. Letago was a quick learner, and soon he was just as strong as his grandfather Khomotso had been.

As the years went by, Kgosi's appealed to rule again but the people had grown tired of his tyranny, and they only wanted for a leader who truly cared about them. Lerato remained on the throne with Letago by her side, Lerato led the Mashita tribe in a rebellion against Kgosi. They fought bravely, using their powers to overcome the enemy. In the end, they emerged victorious, and Kgosi was banished from the tribe forever.

Lerato had achieved what she had set out to do - she had protected her son and reclaimed her rightful place as leader of the Mashita tribe.

Chapter 26: Letago the ruler of Mashita tribe

As Letago grew older, his superpowers became more and more powerful. He was able to control the elements around him with ease, creating strong gusts of wind, summoning lightning bolts, and even controlling the flow of water. His mother, Lerato, knew that he was destined for great things.

One day, a group of explorers from a distant land arrived in Khomotso's village. They were searching for individuals with extraordinary abilities and wanted to take them back to their homeland for further study. Letago was immediately drawn to their strange gadgets and technology, and they were equally fascinated by his powers.

Despite Lerato's reservations, Letago agreed to accompany the explorers on their journey. He was excited to see the world beyond his village and to learn more about his own abilities. However, as they traveled further and further from home, Letago began to realize that these explorers had darker intentions.

They wanted to use Letago's powers for their own gain, to create weapons and tools that could give them an insurmountable advantage in battle. Letago was horrified by their plans, and he knew he needed to escape.

With his powers and quick thinking, Letago managed to outsmart the explorers and flee back to his village. He warned his fellow villagers of the explorers' intentions and together they prepared for battle.

The ensuing fight was intense, but Letago's powers proved to be a valuable asset in their victory. He had found his place in the world, not as a tool to be exploited, but as a protector of his people and their way of life.

Years later, Letago would become known as one of the greatest heroes in his village's history. His story would inspire generations to come, and the legend of Khomotso's family would live on.

Biography

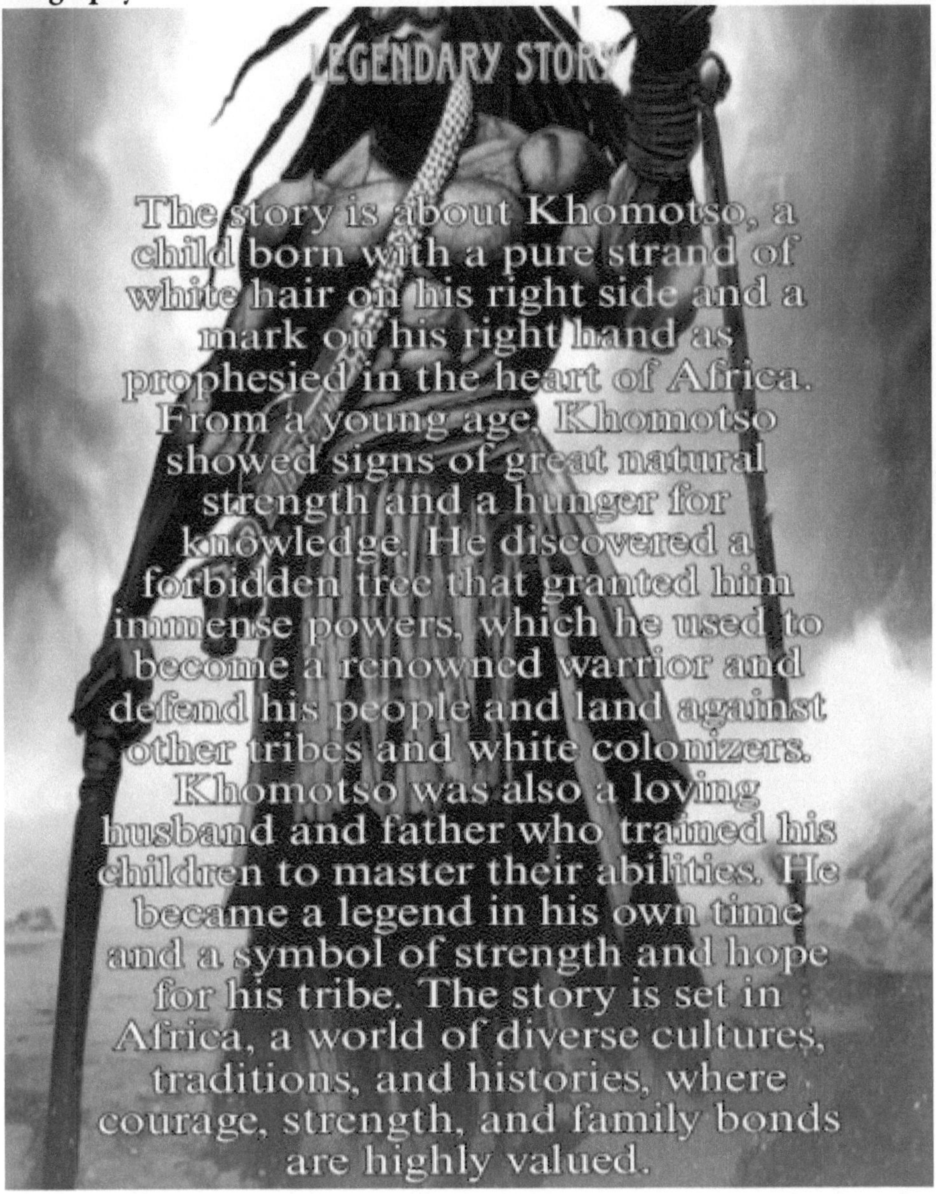

The story is about Khomotso, a child born with a pure strand of white hair on his right side and a mark on his right hand as prophesied in the heart of Africa. From a young age, Khomotso showed signs of great natural strength and a hunger for knowledge. He discovered a forbidden tree that granted him immense powers, which he used to become a renowned warrior and defend his people and land against other tribes and white colonizers. Khomotso was also a loving husband and father who trained his children to master their abilities. He became a legend in his own time and a symbol of strength and hope for his tribe. The story is set in Africa, a world of diverse cultures, traditions, and histories, where courage, strength, and family bonds are highly valued.

KHOMOTJO PETER MASHITA

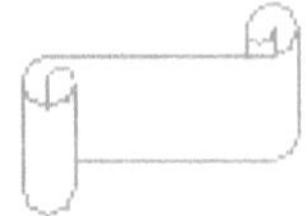

Don't miss out!

Visit the website below and you can sign up to receive emails whenever Khomotjo Peter Mashita publishes a new book. There's no charge and no obligation.

https://books2read.com/r/B-A-EDQX-WQGHC

BOOKS 2 READ

Connecting independent readers to independent writers.